The History of Money

Nicolas Brasch

Australia • Brazil • Japan • Korea • Mexico • Singapore • Spain • United Kingdom • United States

The History of Money

Fast Forward
Blue Level 9

Text: Nicolas Brasch
Illustrations: Margaret Krajnc
Editor: Kate McGough
Design: Vonda Pestana
Series design: James Lowe
Production controller: Emma Hayes
Photo research: Corrina Tauschke
Audio recordings: Juliet Hill, Picture Start
Spoken by: Matthew King and Abbe Holmes
Reprint: Jennifer Foo

Acknowledgements
The author and publisher would like to acknowledge permission to reproduce material from the following sources: Photographs by APL/Corbis/Walter Urie, pp 2, 10; The Art Archive/Dagli Orti (A), cover bottom, pp 1 bottom, 13 top, 13 bottom, 14 top, 14 bottom/ Provinciaal Museum G M Kam/Nijmegen Netherlands/Dagli Orti, cover left inset, pp 1 left inset, 12; Hedgehog House/Colin Monteath, p 9; Istockphoto.com/Tina Rencelj, p 8; Royal Australian Mint, cover right, p 1 right.

ISBN 978 0 17 012534 5
ISBN 978 0 17 012525 3 (set)

Cengage Learning Australia
Level 7, 80 Dorcas Street
South Melbourne, Victoria Australia 3205
Phone: 1300 790 853

Cengage Learning New Zealand
Unit 4B Rosedale Office Park
331 Rosedale Road, Albany, North Shore NZ 0632
Phone: 0800 449 725

For learning solutions, visit **cengage.com.au**

Printed in Australia by Ligare Pty Ltd
7 8 9 10 11 12 13 21 20 19 18 17

Evaluated in independent research by staff from the Department of Language, Literacy and Arts Education at the University of Melbourne.

The History of Money

Nicolas Brasch

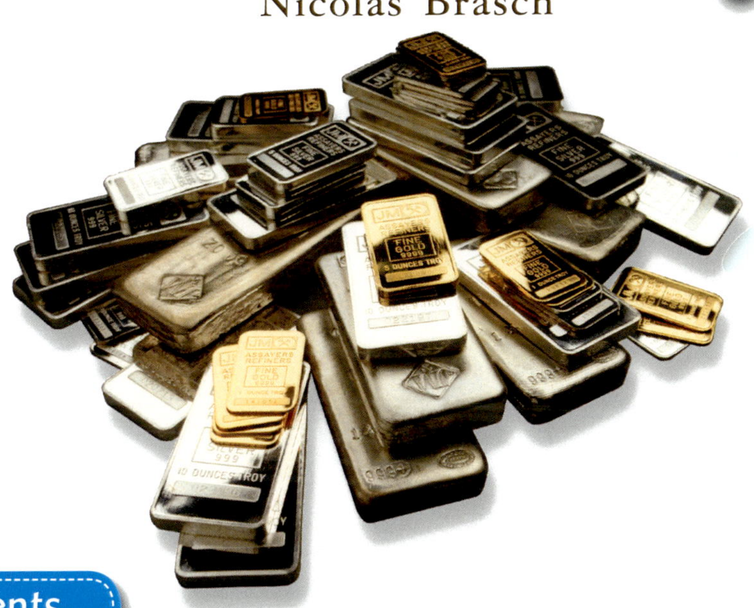

Contents

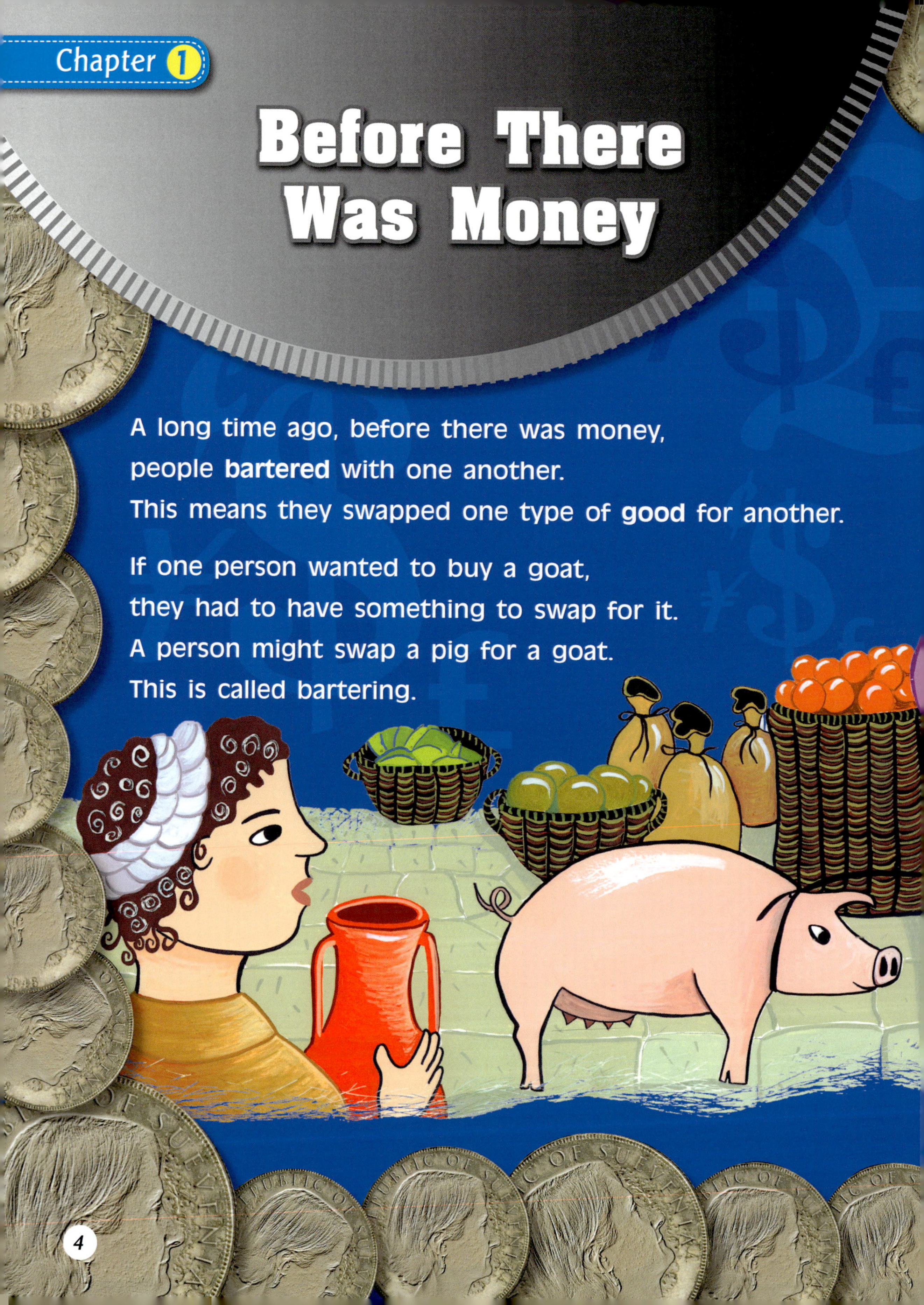

Chapter 1

Before There Was Money

A long time ago, before there was money, people **bartered** with one another. This means they swapped one type of **good** for another.

If one person wanted to buy a goat, they had to have something to swap for it. A person might swap a pig for a goat. This is called bartering.

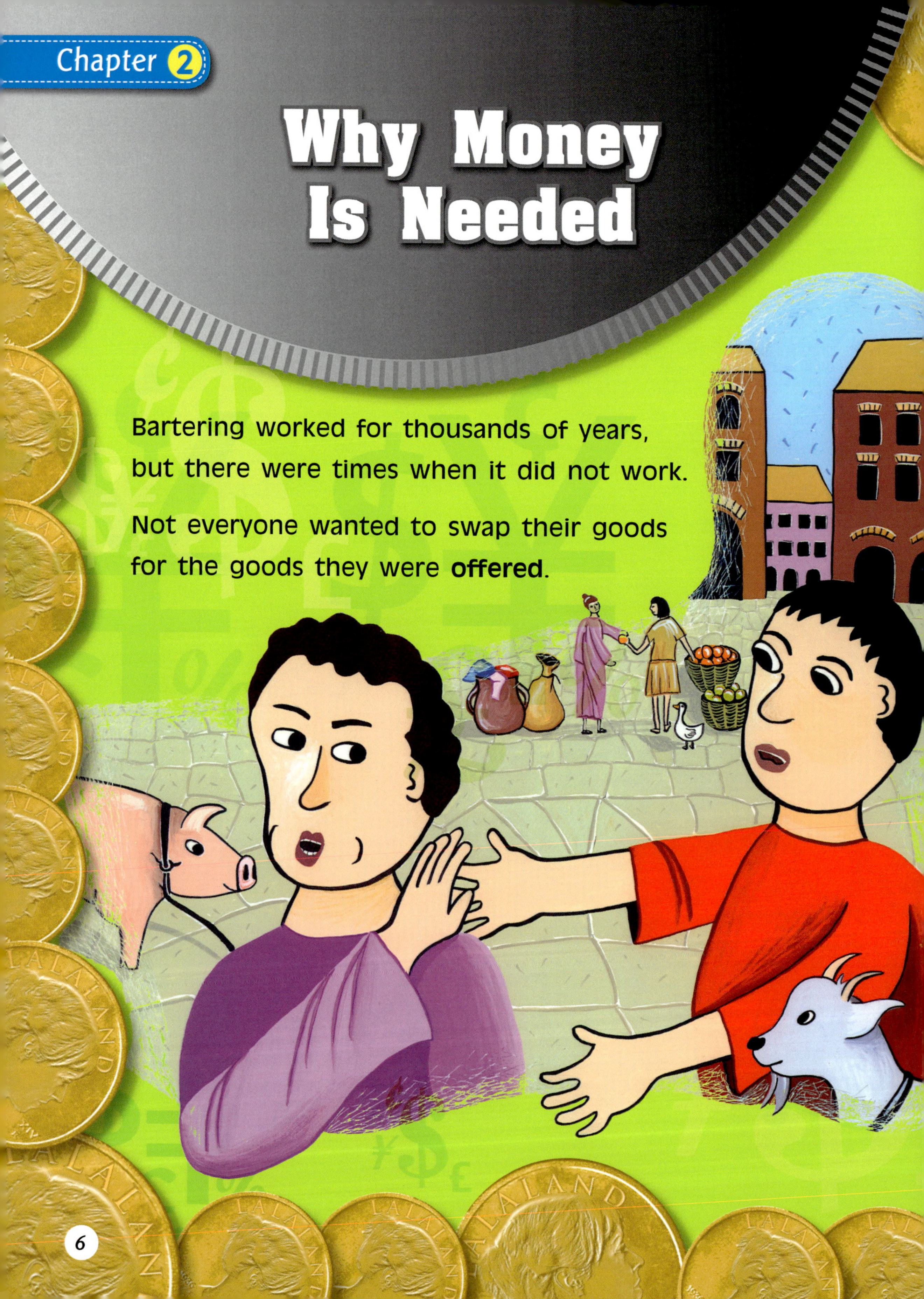

Chapter 2

Why Money Is Needed

Bartering worked for thousands of years, but there were times when it did not work.

Not everyone wanted to swap their goods for the goods they were **offered**.

So another idea was needed.

People needed to find a way to **trade** goods with something that everyone wanted. So the idea of money came about.

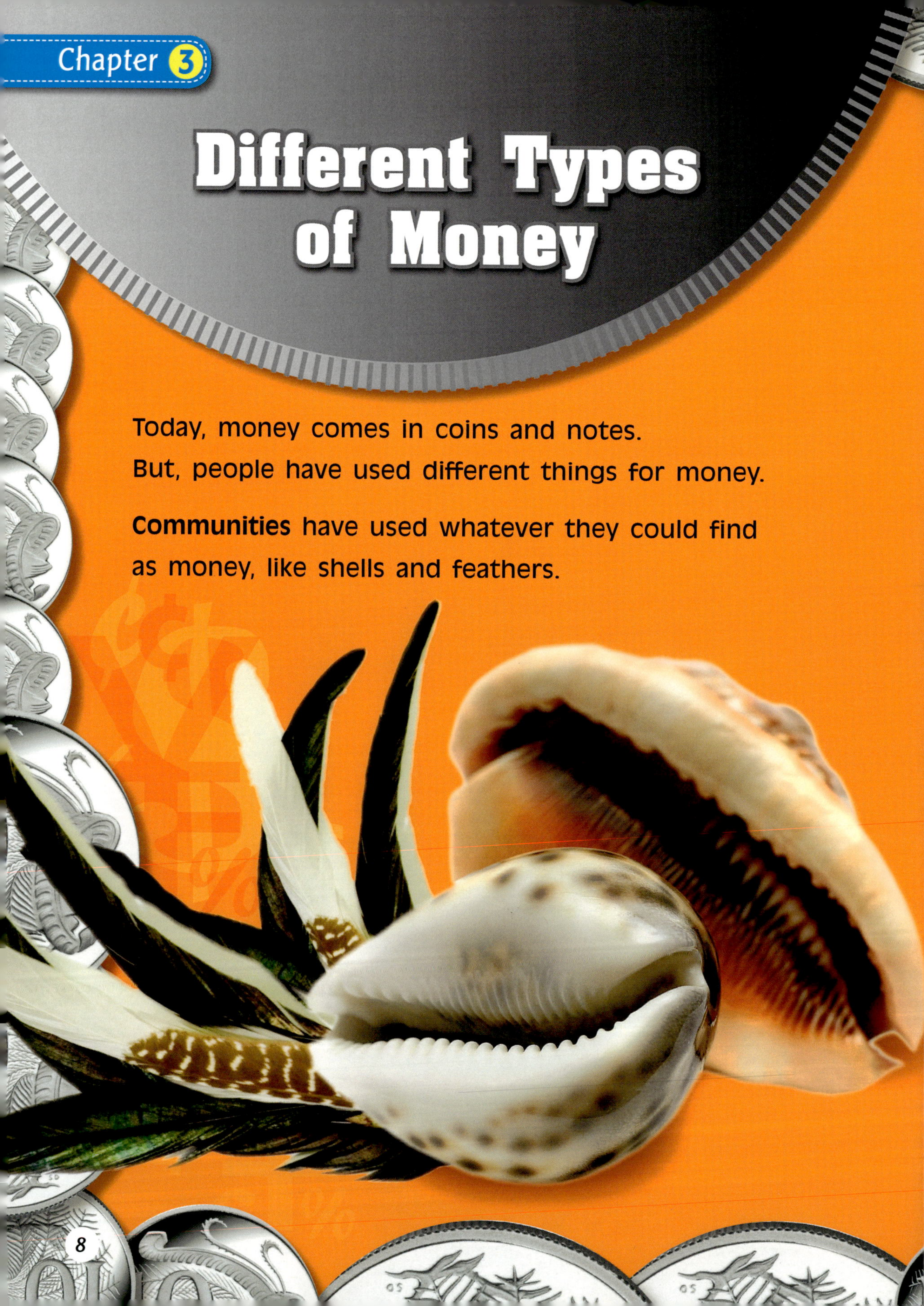

Chapter 3

Different Types of Money

Today, money comes in coins and notes.
But, people have used different things for money.

Communities have used whatever they could find as money, like shells and feathers.

Communities in China used tea bricks.
Tea bricks were small bricks
made by pressing wet tea leaves together.

It did not matter what people used as money,
as long as everyone was happy
to use the same thing.

Most communities in the world used metals as money.
They used **metals** that were very strong.
Strong metal lasts a long time.

Gold and silver are very strong metals.

The strongest metals used were gold and silver. When countries ran out of gold and silver, they went to other countries that had a lot of these metals.

Sometimes, countries swapped goods for gold and silver, and sometimes they just took the metals.

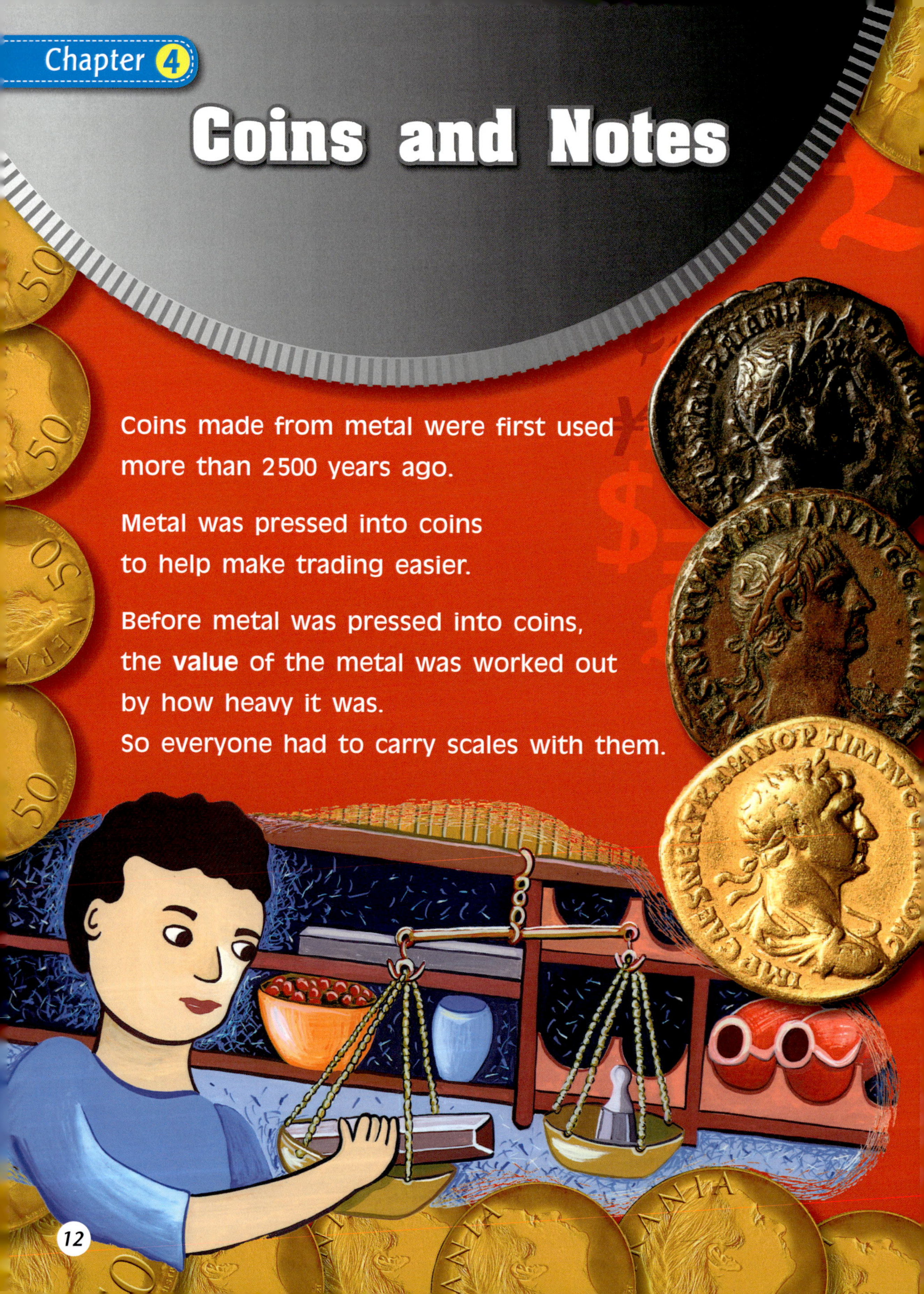

Chapter 4

Coins and Notes

Coins made from metal were first used more than 2500 years ago.

Metal was pressed into coins to help make trading easier.

Before metal was pressed into coins, the **value** of the metal was worked out by how heavy it was. So everyone had to carry scales with them.

Years later, a number was pressed into the metal. People could now see the value of the coin.

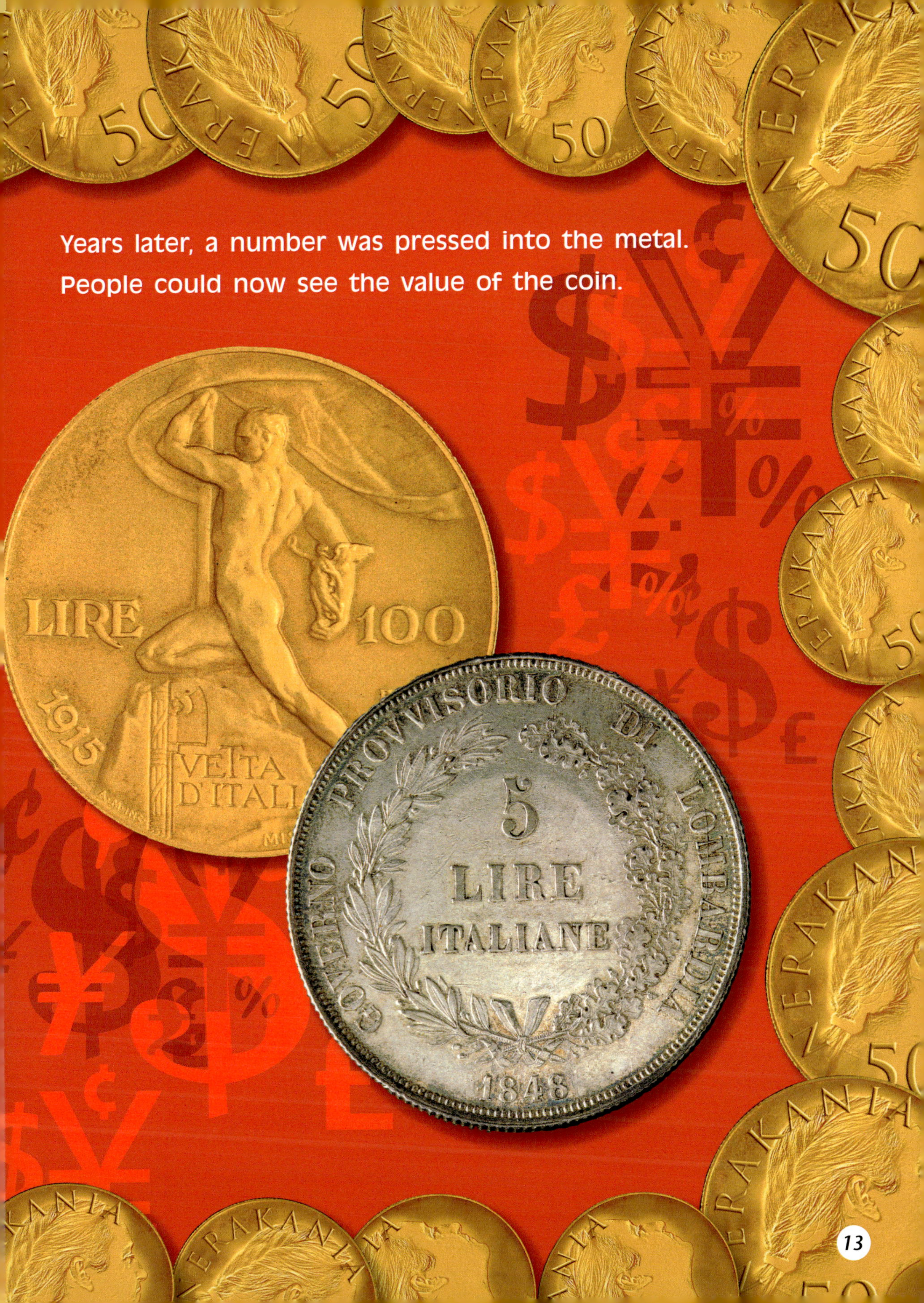

Paper notes were first used as money more than 1000 years ago.

These Chinese paper notes are from the early 1900s.

Paper notes were first used because
coins were heavy to carry around.
If someone wanted to buy goods that cost a lot of money,
they had to carry lots of coins with them.
Paper was a lot easier to carry around.

Glossary

bartered	swapped something for something else
communities	groups of people that live near each other
good	something that can be traded
metals	things such as iron, silver or gold
offered	tried to give something to someone
trade	to buy and sell
value	how much something is

Index